MADHOUSE

MIGUEL ESTRADA

WARNING: This book contains scenes of violence and disturbing themes. Please enjoy at your own discretion.

Table of Contents

CHAPTER 1

At only eleven years old, Lucas would live through all the horrors the human being is capable of. He waved goodbye to his friends as he got off the school bus. The evening air brushed his cheeks and ruffled his brown hair. He walked a couple of blocks to the porch of his house, the smell of freshly cut lawn filling his lungs. The flowers that decorated the entrance shone thanks to the summer warmth.

Lucas decided not to enter through the main door. He liked challenges. From time to time, especially when he was bored, he would find ways to enter without being seen, like a sneaky cat that came and went as he wished.

He used to play hide and seek with his father and friends all the time, and he was always the best—not only because he knew the best places to hide but also because he changed his spots frequently. However, those days were gradually falling behind, especially now that he was in his last days of primary school. By the end of the summer, he would start middle school, so he had to take advantage of what little childhood he had left.

He went around the house into the backyard and found the kitchen door hung wide open. *Too easy*, he told himself. Besides, he risked bumping into someone. He moved on, finding a window to the living room. He tossed a trashcan next to him aside, climbed on top of it, and peeked inside. Nobody home. Perfect.

Lucas had to enter slowly to make sure not to fall headlong onto the floor. He put both hands on the rug, and little by little, he introduced the rest of his body to the living room. Mission accomplished!

He heard voices coming from the kitchen and was glad that he hadn't gone through there. Lucas slid like a shadow to the source of the noise, hoping to jump out and scare the hell out of his parents.

He leaned back against the wall, moving toward the dining room door. There was something strange in their voices. They sounded angry, as if they wanted to scream, but they spoke in whispers instead. He could barely catch snippets of the conversation.

"What are we going to do with him?" his mother Mary asked.

"What do you mean?" replied Tom, his father. "We'll tell him."

"Not yet. I don't think he's ready... I'm not ready..."

"I don't care if you're not ready. He's my son!"

"Both yours and mine."

"Well…"

"Oh, let's not go there, please. Not now."

Lucas came closer. They were obviously talking about him, but what was it that they couldn't tell him?

"I still can't believe you're throwing in the towel so easily," his dad said. "After all these years and all the shit we've been through."

"It's not like we haven't tried, Tom. We've been trying for years, but I'm afraid it's not working."

"I know, I know, but still…"

"Let me ask you a question, and I want you to be as honest as possible. Are you happy?"

Tom remained silent for a moment before answering.

"Of course."

"Let me rephrase the question. Are you happy with me?"

This time, his father did not answer, and Lucas understood what they were talking about. He left his hiding place, trying to hold back the tears.

"No!" he shouted at the top of his lungs, which made his parents jolt in surprise. "You can't split up! We are a family!"

Mary put her hand on her chest with wide eyes and approached him carefully as if she was afraid of touching him.

"Lucas, honey, let me explain..."

"No! There's nothing to explain!"

Lucas stepped back, moving farther away from his mother. Tom just stood there with his arms crossed, nothing to say. He surely knew there was nothing he could say that would calm Lucas at that moment. After all, the boy's world was falling apart.

He had neither uncles nor cousins, and he only saw his grandparents a couple of times a year. He'd always been an only child. His only company, apart from his friends, used to be his pets, which he no longer had. The only family he had were his mom and dad–the pillars that kept the house together and happy. And they were leaving each other.

Lucas had heard the horror stories from his friends whose parents had divorced. Typically, they would live with their mothers through the week. Their dads ended up moving to some small, shabby apartment and could only be visited on weekends.

Lucas didn't want any of that; instead, he wanted to greet them both every day, to dine together at the table and watch TV with them.

"Lucas..." This time it was his father, holding out his hand.

The boy turned and ran straight to his room. He slammed the door behind him and threw himself onto the bed, his face directly on the pillow. He stifled his sobs, without knowing for how long.

Once his eyes had dried, he sat up on his bed. Lucas would teach his parents a lesson. If he were to run away, they would realize how much they loved him and that they could not be a family unless they were together, all of them. Only then would Lucas return, and everybody would be happy again.

The boy stared motionless at the wall for hours as he waited for the night to set his plan in motion.

CHAPTER 2

"You know it has nothing to do with you, right?" Mary asked in a soft voice that caressed his ears; it was the tone she used when she was apologizing for something.

Lucas didn't answer. He was lying down with his gaze fixed on the wall. She sat on the edge of the bed and stroked his hair.

"It's... it's a grown-up thing. Your dad and I still love each other, and we love you too. It's just... it's complicated. Some people are not meant to be together."

"Then why did you get married?"

"Because we loved each other. We still do, but sometimes that's not enough to maintain a relationship. It's like a plant or a pet, you can love it very much, but if you don't take care of it, you risk losing it."

"That sounds stupid."

"Maybe it is, but that's how it works."

"I'm never going to marry," said the boy after a pause.

Mary felt a twinge in her chest.

"Oh, my baby, don't say that. You'll surely find a good woman you'll fall in love with, and raise a happy family together."

"And then, she'll divorce me, and I'll be sad and alone."

Mary let out a sigh. Although Lucas was a bright boy, he was still too young to understand certain things. Besides, he was obviously hurt. Seeing his parents fighting all the time can be toxic to a growing child. In contrast, being divorced didn't sound so bad, if they could get along and share custody. She was sure it was the best route for everyone, yet she knew it would take a long time for him to understand, maybe years.

"Sweetie, I know you feel bad now, but I promise it's not the end of the world. We can still be happy, all three of us. Things will be different from now on, but it's for the best."

Lucas remained silent. Mary leaned over him a little to see him and noticed he had his eyes closed. He was obviously pretending to be asleep so they would stop the conversation. She knew him like the back of her hand. She finished tucking him in and kissed him on the forehead.

"I love you, my prince," she said as she got up from the bed.

Mary hesitated for a second, hoping to hear the "I love you too, my queen," he replied with every night. Only the silence answered.

She crossed the room, put a hand on the knob, ready to close the door behind her, and her fingers instinctively went to the light switch.

"Mom?"

Mary jumped and turned. A hint of hope made her raise her jaw and listen to what he had to say.

"Yes, darling?"

"Remember not to turn off the light," Lucas said as he settled between the sheets.

"Oh, right…"

She jerked her hand away from the switch as if it was hot and gave a timid smile to her son.

"Sweet dreams," said Mary.

This time she didn't wait for him to respond.

CHAPTER 3

Lucas only dared to open his eyes once his mother's footsteps faded away. He knew her routine by heart, but he still had to be careful, especially considering his daring plan. Usually, after putting him to bed, Mary would shower, take her sleeping pills, and then go to bed. His father would stay in the living room watching television until falling asleep. That would be Lucas' opportunity for the perfect escape.

He heard a door closing and then the roar of water gushing out of the shower. Lucas waited for what seemed like an eternity, so long that he had to fight with himself to stay awake. He listened to the whispers outside, which had become more prominent. That just meant that his father was watching one of those western flicks he liked so much.

Once Lucas was sure the shower had stopped, and everything went silent, he decided to get going. He got out of bed and grabbed his backpack. He couldn't help but stare at the water gun resting on the corner, its colors even more striking under the reddish reflection of the lamp. It was one of his favorite toys, the one that helped fight boredom during the summer afternoons he spent with his dad.

Aim higher than where you want to hit, his dad had advised, *remember water falls in a curve.*

Lucas found that it was true after testing it with his friends. Since then, he had paid special attention to any advice his father might've been willing to give him. Although they didn't usually spend a ton of time playing—Tom was an adult and got tired faster—it was something Lucas appreciated a lot. On several occasions, his friends couldn't go out and play. Most of the time, it was because they had to stay in to do their homework, and Lucas, who always completed his homework in time without much effort, stayed alone at home until his father arrived and saved him from boredom. Lucas felt a lump in his stomach as he thought he would no longer have anyone to play with in those situations.

He remembered again what his friends used to tell him about their divorced parents. The uncomfortable silences, the fleeting glances between them, and the growing distance of the two as time passed.

A tear slipped down his cheek, and he was tempted to take the water pistol with him. Maybe it wasn't the most useful thing in the world, but it was worth the extra weight for a good memory. He opened his backpack and slipped in the water pistol as best as he could.

He peered out into the hallway, turning to both sides. No traces of life. He walked down the stairs, placing each foot gently as if he was walking on glass. The slightest creaking of wood could wake his father; it'd happened before when he came down in the middle of the night to drink some water.

Sporadic blue flashes from the television reflected on the wall. The whispers had become a conversation between the characters in an old western movie, just as Lucas had expected, accompanied by his father's snoring. The sofa was facing the television, its back turned to the stairs, and Lucas saw the outline of his father's head tilted to the side and approached. He put his feet on the carpet, first the heel, and then the rest of the foot, thus reducing the noise drastically.

Lucas reached the entrance and tried to turn the knob, but it didn't move. He took the lock off, and a metallic click startled him. He turned to where his father was and saw him squirming on the couch.

Stay sleep, please, stay sleep, he thought.

Tom finally settled, and, after a few seconds, the snoring returned. Lucas sighed with relief and turned the knob again. This time it gave.

He opened the door and crossed the threshold into the street, or rather, into a new life.

CHAPTER 4

Lucas wasn't afraid of the night. It was the darkness that made all of the hairs on his body stand on end. Thankfully, he didn't have to worry about it at the moment, since all of the streets were brightly lit. Even some of the buildings whose occupants had left hours earlier still kept their lights on, showing abandoned rooms and offices. It comforted him a little; he liked the silence. Not to mention the open space, which could be appreciated much better when no one walked the streets. The damp, cold air blew his hair and forced him to put his hands in his pockets.

While there were some alleyways where the light didn't reach, Lucas sought comfort in the fact that his parents would now have to put their differences aside in order to find him. Once they were back together as a family, he would return, and everybody would be happy again. The goal now was to figure out where to go. Calling one of his friends was not an option. If he did, their parents would ask about his mom or dad and whether or not they would allow him to stay the night. Why did adults always want to have control over everything?

His thoughts were interrupted by a wave of hot air that struck him from the side, accompanied by the roar of an engine. From the corner of his eye, he saw a black figure quickly pass by. A car. The taillights turned a brilliant crimson while slowing to a full stop.

Weird, he thought, but he continued on his way. He began to notice several things as he approached. The car's windows were tinted, so black that it was impossible to see through, which made him wonder how the driver could see at night. The second thing was the absence of a rear license plate. That disturbed him a bit; it was like someone who covered his face in public. However, the car probably had a license plate on the front, and the one on the back had simply fallen off or something.

The car was still on the road as Lucas walked beside it. He did his best to hide his concern. Once he could see the front, he saw that it didn't have a license plate either. The vehicle's headlights shone brightly, menacingly, like two threatening eyes watching him. The engine trembled, giving the impression that it had a life of its own.

Lucas looked away and stepped up his pace. He could see from the corner of his eye that the black car had started to follow him. It moved slowly, matching his speed as if it were an obedient pet. Lucas didn't like that at all. He felt the impulse to run away, but he controlled himself. Whoever was in the vehicle hadn't done anything wrong, and if he ran, he risked getting chased. Lucas walked past an alley on his right, which invited him to take refuge, but it was so dark that he couldn't see the other side, and the last thing he wanted was to be trapped in the dark.

He took a deep breath and saw that, on the other side of the street, there was an intersection that led to another avenue, and it was so narrow the car could not pass through.

Lucas started to jog, picking up momentum, and then ran as fast as he could to the intersection. He reached the other side, where he was greeted by a neighborhood that ended on a dead-end street. The chilly air stirred the beads of sweat on his forehead as he ran. He reached the other side of the road and rested his hands on his knees as he recovered his breath.

He rose, still panting. A golden flash blinded him and forced him to cover his eyes with his forearm. It was the same black car.

Panicking, he lunged in the opposite direction as he heard the wheels grinding against the asphalt, picking up speed. He reached the end of the street and stopped in front of a wall. Lucas closed his eyes, waiting for the impact of the metal to crush his bones against the wall, but nothing happened.

He opened them slowly and turned around.

The car's door was wide open. A silhouetted figure faced him on the driver's side; he couldn't make out a face, and what he heard took him by surprise.

"What are you doing out so late?" A female voice asked. "Are you by yourself?"

"Y-yes," Lucas replied, barely aware that his voice was shaking.

"Where are your parents?" Asked the woman, who seemed like an angelic being under the light.

"They... they're not around..." Lucas answered.

"Come on. You shouldn't be alone outside, it's dangerous."

Don't talk to strangers! Shouted his mother's voice from the recesses of his mind.

"Can you turn down the lights, please?" Lucas asked, eyes narrowed.

"Oh, of course!" she replied and disappeared for a moment. The lights turned off, and she came out again. Now he could see her clearly.

She was beautiful, as much as a woman in her fifties could be, tall and thin with black hair that fell on her shoulders almost to her waist, her face so white, contrasting with the night and matching her blouse.

"Want me to give you a ride?" The woman in white asked.

Don't!

"Shut up, Mom," Lucas mumbled and walked over to the lady.

"What did you say?" She asked.

"Nothing."

Lucas approached the car. The woman gave him a broad smile that showed a row of perfect white teeth and dimpled her cheeks. Lucas could not help but blush and smile back.

"I am Bella," she said, offering her hand. He shook it, realizing that, although soft, her grip was as firm as a man's.

"L-Lucas," said the boy.

"Nice to meet you, Lucas."

Bella led him to the passenger seat and opened the door. He stepped in and fastened his seat belt while eyeing the car. It looked old, even a bit worn, but well maintained, the seats giving off a sweet smell he could not identify. He looked in the back seats for some food residue the lady might have left, but there was nothing. She took a seat, got ready, and started driving.

"Sorry about the smell," said Bella. "I'm just back from buying groceries."

There were no bags in the backseats. Maybe she put everything in the trunk.

"I don't want to go home," Lucas confessed.

"I'm glad," said Bella. "We're not going to your house."

"Good!"

"Why don't you want to go back?"

"My parents don't love each other anymore," Lucas said with a lump in his throat. "I don't think... I don't think they love me anymore either."

"Don't think like that," said Bella "You deserve to be loved. To grow in a nice and happy family."

He felt something warm slip down his cheek. The reflection in the window revealed that it was a tear, and he wiped it with his wrist as he nodded.

"What if I were to adopt you?" Bella asked as she turned her head to him waiting for an answer. "I live with my husband and his mom. I'm sure you'll love it with us." Lucas opened his mouth to reply but was interrupted. "Could you pass me something in the glove compartment?"

He obeyed, reached in and found a blue surgical mask.

"You mean this?"

"Yes, exactly."

He gave it to her and noticed they had slowed down while she was putting it on.

"What's that for?" He asked.

"You'll see." Bella turned on the air conditioner.

The grilles blew a frigid air so powerful it made him blink. Lucas began to feel light-headed and his vision blurred. Before he could even wonder what was going on, his head slammed against the window, his eyes closing against his will. The last thing he heard was Bella's distant voice:

"Goodnight."

CHAPTER 5

A sharp pain ran through Lucas's head, from the temples to the forehead, so intense that he could feel his eyes coming out of their sockets. He blinked several times as he tried to make sense of what was around him. He was lying down, looking up toward a gray ceiling with black spots and cobwebs in the corners. A light bulb hung on a bare wire, emitting a faint yellowish light. The bed he was laying on smelled of urine; the sheets were pale blue with drawings of horses galloping. The walls must have been painted pink a long time ago, but now they were covered in a pale white with little traces of worn color that spread like crumpled paper. It was a girl's room; that he was sure of, or at least it must have been at some point.

The last things he remembered were two lights watching him like God's judging eyes. A car's headlights, a beautiful woman—but there was something strange about her. She had lied to him; she had said that she had just come back from buying groceries, but there were no bags in the backseats. Then… goodnight.

Lucas got up suddenly, with something hard and cold wrapped around his wrist, pulling him. He removed the sheet and found himself handcuffed to the edge of the bed. His heartbeat quickened as he started screaming without realizing it.

He tried to force his hand out without any success. The wood of the bed creaked every time he pulled. His eyes scanned the place for something he could use to free himself. He had no idea how he would accomplish such a feat, but he had to try before the crazy lady returned. With his free hand, he patted the mattress, finding nothing but yellow, deflated pillows.

Heavy footsteps coming from outside made him stop; they were not Bella's. They were so loud that he could almost feel the house shaking with every step. Whoever it was, it was someone big. Instinctively, Lucas covered himself with the sheets and closed his eyes.

The door creaked open, and a putrid smell made its way through his nostrils. It was a mixture of alcohol and something sweet, just like what he had smelled in the car.

"Rise and shine, champ," said a rough voice.

Slowly, Lucas opened his eyes. A blurry figure in front of him began to take shape. He had been right about his size; the man was huge. He looked seven feet tall, with broad shoulders and pale skin. He wore a blue button-down shirt, with spots and wrinkles, and khaki pants that seemed to have suffered decades of abuse. However, the most dismal thing about him was his face, which was framed by a thick white beard and a bald head that shone under the bulb's light. His black eyes looked like a dead man's.

"Who are you trying to trick?" The man asked. "I heard you scream, and now you want me to believe you've been sleeping?"

Lucas tried to say something, but only meaningless babbling came out of his mouth.

"What did you say, son?" The man asked, drawing closer.

"W-Where am I?"

"You are at home." The man sat on the edge of the bed and fixed his dead gaze on Lucas; a wide, creepy smile appeared on his face. "We're your new family now."

Lucas felt a knot in his stomach, and his eyes got wet. The boy pursed his lips, suppressing his desire to scream for help. He swallowed, and his trembling mouth mumbled a question.

"C-can you take off the handcuffs...? My wrist hurts."

The man's grim smile faded and gave way to a shadowed look. Lucas held his breath. The guy's hand went to the back of his pants, and Lucas waited for him to pull out a key, but it wasn't. He heard the sound of metal scraping, and the orange light in the room reflected on the edge of a knife.

"You're not going to be a smartass with me, are you?" The man whispered.

Lucas shook his head as hard as he could without taking his eyes off the knife. His heart was pounding so fast it seemed about to burst from his chest. The man stabbed the nightstand beside him, and the knife bit into the wood without any effort.

Lucas stared at the blade with wide eyes. It was formidable, surely made to cut meat and unlike anything else in the place, it was impeccable, so much so that he could see his own inverted reflection. A bunch of keys collided with each other in a tinkle, and he felt the man's grip on his wrist. The man's hands were enormous and hard as stone.

"There," the man said while inserting a small key in the handcuffs. There was a click, and they opened. Lucas took out his hand and began to rotate it to relieve the tension. "I like you, no buzz and no whining.

It tells me that you'll be a good addition to the family, unlike the brats that have come before you. I cut a finger off the last girl that got me mad with that knife you see right there. Just be good and don't piss me off."

Lucas nodded.

"My name is Martin, by the way, Martin Anderson, but from now on you'll call me Dad, so it doesn't matter much."

Martin stood up. He seemed to be the size of a building from the bed.

"T-Thank you..." Lucas muttered as he stroked his wrist with his shaking hand.

"You're welcome, son," Martin replied with a surprisingly calm tone.

Martin grabbed the knife and snatched it off the table. He went to the door and put his hand on the switch.

"No!" Lucas cried.

Martin slowly turned over his shoulder. Lucas looked down before his gaze bumped into Martin's.

"Please, don't turn off the light..."

The boy waited for Martin to yell at him, or to throw the knife straight into his eye, but none of those horrible things happened.

"Fine," said Martin. "If that's what'll take to keep you quiet."

Martin slammed the door behind him, and everything in the room shook. Lucas let out a sigh of relief. He waited for the footsteps to fade away and cautiously got out of bed.

This can't be happening. This has to be a nightmare, and I have to wake up.

He didn't wake up. He could see every detail around him, breathe every smell, and feel a fear like he had never felt before. Every time he had nightmares, he would always wake up in the worst part. The fact he was still here proved that this wasn't a dream and that his only hope was to escape. It couldn't be very difficult, could it? After all, he had done it once before; the only difference was that this time, he didn't have to fool his parents, but rather a pair of psychopaths who would do something much worse than grounding him.

Lucas looked around until he found a window. He tried to open it, using all of his strength, but it only rose a few inches. He wiped the sweat from his forehead and tried again. The window finally relented, reaching the top, and he received a wave of the soft air of the night.

Lucas had to restrain himself from crying out in victory. His joy didn't last long.

He put both hands on the ledge and peered out. Perpetual darkness returned his gaze. Lucas couldn't see anything beyond a couple of feet away, only a faded roof that had already lost several slabs. Trying to jump from there would be suicide or, at best, lead to a broken leg. He couldn't risk it. If he wanted to make it out in one piece, he would need all his bones intact. Not to mention the fact that there wasn't a single light source outside that didn't come from the house itself. For a second, he wondered what would be worse, being trapped in that madhouse or jumping into the unknown. He didn't want to know the answer.

Lucas stepped back and tried to focus his attention on something else. He noticed that his backpack was in the corner of the room, surrounded by a bunch of broken dolls. He grabbed one of the straps and lifted it. A bright orange and green object came out of the opening and crashed to the ground with a bang. It was the water gun. For some reason, the backpack had been opened before he woke, and whoever did it left everything inside it.

He was just starting his escape, and things were already going south. It didn't take long for him to hear the steps again, and they were coming fast.

His first instinct was to jump into the bed and pretend to sleep again, but Martin didn't fall for that trick the first time around. He ran to the bed and settled as many pillows as he could under the sheets, making sure the silhouette looked like someone in a fetal position. Meanwhile, the footsteps became louder; the ground beneath his feet began to tremble.

Lucas finished his work and got into the closet behind him. He left the door ajar so he could peek out. At that moment, the door burst open, hit the wall and bounced back, but Martin stopped it before it closed again, pushing it aside.

The giant walked over to the bed and leaned just above the dummy of pillows. He watched it carefully without moving as if expecting Lucas to jump out of bed. He held the knife in his left hand, gripped with such force that his knuckles turned white, the veins of his forearm about to explode.

Lucas waited. He was sure Martin would stab the pillows and see a bunch of feathers come out instead of blood. Full of rage, the man would go down to look for Lucas all over the house. Lucas would then make a run for the front door and reach the street, calling for help. Someone would see a child running away from a psychopath with a knife and come to his rescue. It wasn't a perfect plan, but it was the only one he had.

However, Martin remained inert for a while longer. The seconds became minutes, and Lucas was sure that the walls inside the closet were getting closer. He began to breathe deeply and slowly as he felt the air running out. He would suffocate, surrounded by a heap of hideous coats.

Just when he thought he couldn't stand a second more in that little hell, Martin stepped back, turned around, and walked towards the exit. He looked over his shoulder a couple of times before leaving and closed the door.

Lucas let out a sigh of relief and stepped out of the closet. All he could hear was a whistle coming from his own eardrum—the unmistakable sign of silence.

He decided to leave the backpack in the room. If any of the Andersons came to check and noticed it wasn't there, they would remove the sheets and see that he had escaped. Besides, nothing he had would be really useful.

With his heart still pounding, Lucas opened the door and ventured into the hallway.

CHAPTER 6

The wallpaper ran along the edges with stripes that zigzagged along, exposing the dirty gray with which the walls had originally been painted. It seemed as if the cobwebs around it were the only things that kept the paper from peeling off. The photographs that rested on the shelves had a brown tone, and they all displayed the happy couple; some in the park, some at a wedding. In one of them, Bella Anderson was wearing a white dress that slid to the floor like a waterfall. As a young girl, she looked just as beautiful, with a smile that promised a fairy tale ending. Obviously, that was not what she got. The pictures were nothing but memories corroded by time.

However, Lucas noticed that one of the frames was shattered; a piece of the photograph had been torn out. He walked towards it, with his nose almost touching the frame. It showed Martin, wearing a button-up shirt, with his arm around his wife's shoulder, who was wearing a flower dress that made her look younger than she probably was. They were both smiling, staring at the missing piece. There used to be someone there, a ghost that was erased from their memories.

The creaking of wood made him turn his head. Nothing. Probably a moan of pain old houses make. As a child, when his grandmother was still alive, they often visited her at her mansion on the outskirts of the city, and he would always be scared of the noises he heard in the middle of the night. His father used to reassure him, telling him it was some pipe, a piece of loose wood, or a gust of wind. He had explained that this was often the case in old houses.

They're like old people, he had said. *Sometimes they hurt their hips, sometimes they hurt their joints, and they whine in pain. Houses are like that, and when you spend a lot of time without taking good care of them, they start to wear out.*

And it was obvious the house was not well maintained. The light bulb in the hallway barely produced a faint glow, so he had to squint to see where he was walking, but it was enough. He was fine as long as he could see what was in front of him. The problem was when he was surrounded by total darkness, as if being swallowed by it. When even having his eyes open wide felt the same as having them closed. That's what terrified him; not knowing what might be lurking in the shadows. A shiver ran through his body, and he forced himself not to think about it.

Lucas continued down the hallway until he found a set of stairs. As he went down toward the dining room, the same sweet smell flooded his senses. Wide windows covered the place, with only blackness visible on the other side. Lucas came up to see his own reflection on the glass and tried to open them without any success. All of them were tightly sealed; those psychos had made sure no one could get out.

Lucas glanced around with the faint hope of finding something to throw and break the glass with, but he reconsidered. Breaking the windows would make a lot of noise, and he could not risk being discovered. Besides, he had to take into account that he would not be able to see anything once outside. He would be blind, prowling aimlessly over terrain he didn't know, and his pursuers would eventually catch him. His heart quickened at the thought. Maybe he could escape through the garage; he would just have to get the remote to open the door. However, he didn't know where to even begin looking. There was no choice. The front door was his only way out.

He peered out into the hallway again and crossed a corner. He found a door and pushed it gently. The rusting hinges creaked in tune, a song that gave him goosebumps.

The lobby was huge; probably a small apartment could fit in there. In the center, there was a set of furniture facing a big television; its black screen reflected the whole place. A round table in the middle served as a dumping ground for whatever was left from the Anderson's movie marathons. There were empty bags of sweets and dirty, sticky dishes that had become the home of several insects. At the sides of the hall, stairs led up to a platform on the second floor connecting the rooms upstairs. He was astounded by how elegant this place could become, leaving aside the mess the Andersons had left.

On the other side of the room, Lucas could see a double wooden door. His heart started pounding again, this time with excitement. He was so close, and yet so far. He just had to walk there, open the doors, and find the way back to the road without being discovered. That was key; he didn't want to even imagine what would happen if the Andersons found out. The mere thought of the butcher knife gave him shivers.

Lucas walked in long strides, with nervous eyes that saw everything around him, alert to any movement. Finally, he reached the entrance, put his hand on the cold knob, and turned it, but it didn't budge.

He tried to turn it around again. It wasn't moving. He put both hands on each knob and pulled it as hard as he could, with the faint hope that it would burst open and push him back, but the door held steady.

Lucas gave up and stood there for a while; his eyes fixed on his only way out. He clenched his fists as his eyes watered with impotence. He wanted to scream, but the part of his brain in charge of his survival forced him to bite his lips and swallow his frustration.

He needed a key if he wanted to get out, nothing more and nothing less. That reassured him a little. The task was simple: get the key and get out of there.

Where had he seen one? The faint image of a silver key jumped on his mind, but was it a memory trying to show him what had happened in the lapse of time he had fainted? Or just trickery from his imaginative mind? He closed his eyes, unsure if that would help, but he did it anyway, trying to remember what had happened before he fainted.

There was nothing but a thick mist in his mind. Instead of trying to remember, he focused on figuring out the problem. Most people kept an extra set of keys in the garage or someplace where they could get it easily. If he were lucky, he would find it. Lucas went back as cautiously as he had come, so close to freedom and not wanting to spoil it with a stupid decision.

Lucas expected to see Martin at every corner, his eyes bulging and his smile wide and twisted. There were two doors near the dining room; door number one was locked, and number two was just a small closet for the mops and cleaning products the Andersons had clearly stopped using years ago. He decided to go to the kitchen.

As he entered, he noticed a pigeon's body lying in the sink with its legs up, its feathers entangled with each other, and its neck twisted back in an impossible way. So that was the source of the smell. He couldn't help but gag at the sight.

While staying as far away from the bird as possible, Lucas inspected each of the drawers. He found only expired products and rusted silverware. He bent down and opened a double cabinet. Several bottles of cleaning products came into view. Right at the end of the line, he spotted a bottle of bleach. Once, when he was younger, he had grabbed a bottle of bleach out of curiosity. His mom caught him in the act and lost her temper, screaming that he could go blind by touching it. At the time, he didn't see the connection between touching the bottle and going blind. Over the years he realized that he could be blinded if the bleach went in his eyes.

Lucas got up and headed for the exit, ready to continue his search elsewhere, when he heard a metallic shriek behind him. Out of the corner of his eye, he saw a white figure leaning over something. His heart stopped for a moment. He turned to see an old woman, reclining in her wheelchair, with her dead eyes fixed on him, and for a moment they seemed to have gone wider as if she was surprised to see him there.

From her open mouth, a thin thread of saliva hung into her lap. He wanted to beg with her to keep quiet, but the words never came out of his mouth.

The old woman lifted one of her decrepit fingers toward him. Lucas felt his world fall apart as if the ground had opened in a bottomless pit. He waited for the woman to scream with all the strength of her worn-out lungs. However, she remained silent, staring expectantly for a couple of seconds that seemed to linger for an eternity, inert as a statue. The only sign that she was still alive was her threatening finger; then he understood...

Lucas turned slowly, afraid his neck would make a sound if he moved it too fast. The lady wasn't pointing at him but at the hallway behind him. Martin was walking with his shoulder against the wall as if fearing to fall to the side. In his hand, he carried a half-finished bottle.

Lucas moved quickly to the side of the kitchen and pressed his back against the wall, hiding behind the door. Martin didn't see him, thank God.

The old woman put her finger back on the arm of the wheelchair, and Lucas was nearly overwhelmed with gratitude.

You're not like them, he thought. *When I get out of here, I'll look for help and make sure they take you to a better place.*

He heard Martin's heavy boots smash the ground, growing closer. The smell of liquor made Lucas frown. He bent down and pressed his body further into the wall. Martin's gigantic head swiveled and came to rest on the woman.

"You okay, ma?" Martin growled.

The old woman nodded, the movement of her head was barely perceptible. Lucas tried to keep his eyes on the ground, afraid that if he dared to look at Martin, the man would feel his gaze. But curiosity got the best of him, and he raised his head almost against his own will. Half of Martin's torso was visible, and on his waist, he carried a bunch of keys that collided with one another in a metallic symphony. Lucas had to bite his tongue so as not to let out a gasp.

"Well, I'm going to watch TV. If you see something funky going on, you tell me, is that clear?"

Martin's mother nodded again, and he left. Lucas let the air trapped in his lungs escape; he had been holding his breath without realizing it. He slowly stood up and noticed that his clothes were stuck to his skin by sweat.

That had been too close, and now he had to go even deeper into the wolf's mouth.

CHAPTER 7

With the stealth of a cat, Lucas followed Martin through the corridor, his head lowered and his knees bent almost to a crouch.

Martin dragged his feet on the floor as he staggered, mumbling meaningless phrases with occasional swears. The bottle that hung between his fingers threatened to fall and crash. He brought it to his lips and took a long, deep gulp followed by a burp.

The drunken man stopped dead in his tracks. Lucas imitated him, his eyes wide. Martin couldn't have heard him; he hadn't made any noise. Lucas glanced around, desperate for a hiding place. Anywhere he could fit his tiny body would serve, but he only found a few shelves with photographs and paintings on the walls that stared at him indifferently.

Lucas wanted to run away, but he stepped back instead, each step as delicate as the ones he had taken to get there. Martin began to move his head to the side. Lucas covered his mouth with one hand and waited for the worst.

Martin did not finish turning, focusing his attention on the corridor to his left. He put the bottle on a little table that rested in the corner and went on his way.

Lucas stifled a sob. He had never been so afraid in his life. The night had to end soon. There was no way he could take the keys without Martin noticing. All he could do was wait for Martin to fall asleep or pass out drunk, but that could take hours, and waiting so long was a luxury he couldn't afford, not when his life was at stake.

Besides, he still had not run into Bella. He was grateful for that, but he knew that, sooner or later, his luck would run out. That witch had hypnotized him somehow. The last thing he remembered was getting into her car, and the next, Martin was threatening him with a butcher knife.

Maybe she was asleep, and that was why he hadn't bumped into her. She had probably gone to bed to avoid seeing her trophy husband all messed up. But it didn't make sense. They seemed to be the kind of people who stayed up all night because they couldn't sleep. Such disturbed minds should not be able to rest, should they?

Then it came to him, like a revelation from heaven. His mother took pills to sleep. If Bella used something similar, she should have a capsule stored in a restroom somewhere. He'd take a few and put them in Martin's bottle. At best, the giant would fall into such a deep sleep that he wouldn't notice Lucas taking away his keys. In the worst case, well, he knew it was not a good idea to mix pills with alcohol.

Just thinking about the possibility that he would hurt someone, even a person as bad as Martin, made his stomach turn.

"Only two pills," Lucas whispered to himself. "Only two, and he'll just sleep."

Lucas returned. With each door he passed, he lay down with his cheek on the floor to see if the wood gave way to ceramic slabs. He didn't want to open a door and find someone he shouldn't.

Finally, after an exhaustive search, Lucas found the door he was looking for, he opened it and found himself in a small bathroom. The toilet was yellow with brown water stains that slid down the side, no lid, and a rusty chain hung out of it. The place where the bathtub was supposed to be was empty, with dripping metal pipes protruding from holes. The sink was broken in half, and black water dripped. There were no mirrors or drawers to store anything.

Lucas let out a snort of frustration and headed down the hallway again until he found a larger space—a second room. It had no TV, but a couple of worn sofas and a staircase that went up to a second-floor section disconnected from the rest. He went up, and a cockroach greeted him, crawling around a corner and moving its antennae up and down. A shiver ran through Lucas's spine as he stepped aside in disgust.

At the top, he found a wall dividing two paths. The right led to a kind of balcony, and on the left, there was a hallway lit by an old blinking lamp.

Both dark paths—both inviting him into the unknown.

CHAPTER 8

The flickering bulb of the lamp threatened to go out at any moment. Lucas could not help but stare at it. The switches did not work, so he didn't dare to venture that way, as he ran the risk of being trapped in the shadows, blind and vulnerable to any attack. He decided to go to the right, where the path opened onto a balcony that served as a corridor. The lights worked there, but they were dim and barely lit the way; the darkness of the night enveloped everything else.

Lucas moved across the balcony, hugging the wall, the wood creaking beneath his feet. Perhaps on the side of the rail, the floor would be more stable. He swallowed hard, his eyes went up, afraid to look into the darkness below, but he caught a flash out of the corner of his eye.

A pale woman moved like a ghost through the bushes outside. Her black hair ruffled over her face, but Lucas could guess that it was Bella.

She carried a flashlight in one hand and pushed the bushes out of her way with the other.

A spectral sob pierced his ears, and the hairs all over his body rose at the same time. It was a cry that echoed with grief and horror at the same time. He couldn't believe that something like that could come from a human being. He would have imagined it coming from a ghost out of a scary movie, like the ones he wasn't supposed to watch before bed.

Lucas returned to the wall so that he could see only the top of the woman's head and felt a hint of relief. She would not be able to see him there even if she dared to look up. He finally reached the entrance that led back to the corridors and entered it. The lamps were also lit up there, but he could still see the light blinking in the adjacent hallway.

He bent down until his cheek touched the cold floor and peeked under the door. There were four wooden legs and some tables. It must've been the master bedroom, so he moved on. If they were anything like his parents, they would have the pills in the bathroom. He knew that expecting a crazy couple to behave like everybody else was absurd, yet he had no choice but to hope for the best. He bent down again in front of another door and saw a blue ceramic floor and a white base that should be the toilet. Bingo.

He stepped into the bathroom, turned on the light, and closed the door behind him. A sweet, metallic scent struck his nose. Lucas frowned and covered his face with his forearm. He lifted the lid off the toilet. Clean. He approached the blue curtain that covered the tub. He didn't want to see the source of that smell; surely it was coming from something disgusting, like everything else in that house, but an invisible force moved his hand and pulled the curtain to the side.

The tub was filled almost to the top with a crimson substance. Blood—a lot of it. Red spatters decorated the white walls. Lucas took a few steps back until his back hit the door. He couldn't avoid gagging again and felt a tickle all over his body as he imagined all that blood spurting out of him.

Lucas jumped toward the curtain and closed it. He waited a moment while the urge to vomit subsided, then he leaned against the sink and looked at his own reflection in the mirror. His eyes were red and damp, his face so pale that he blended in with the wall behind him.

He opened the cabinet behind the mirror and found several bottles of pills. The labels showed such complicated names that he doubted anyone who didn't have a Ph.D. could even pronounce them. All were full.

Someone doesn't want to take what the shrink recommended, he thought.

And then he saw it, a familiar bottle at the top, different from the rest since it was the only one that was almost empty. He put a foot on the toilet lid, and his hand on the sink to push himself up to reach for it. There were only a few pills left in the bottle.

Lucas left the bathroom as he put the bottle in his pocket and wondered which way to take back. He didn't want to be so close to getting caught again, but going through the creepy corridor with that flickering light wasn't appealing either.

He peered down the hall, hoping the path would be shorter so he would only have to run to the other side before the light went out.

And there it was. His salvation.

He was surprised that he hadn't noticed it before. Maybe he was so focused on that faulty lamp that he never saw what was on the side table: a telephone.

Lucas's heart began to beat so fast it felt like a buzzing. He could call for help, get the police, and this whole nightmare would end.

But the lamp, that stupid lamp turning on and off as if mocking him, threatening him. *Just go for it*, it said, *then I'll turn off and leave you alone in the dark.*

"I have to try," he told himself.

He waited for a few seconds and calculated how long it took to switch on and off. It was every thirty seconds, enough to run, make the call and leave, right? But if the person on the other side of the telephone took a while to respond, what would he do then? He didn't want to find out, he shook the thought out of his mind and counted: 3... 2... 1...

The light bulb turned on, and Lucas ran. His hand reached and grabbed the phone before the rest of him noticed. He put it on his ear and heard the beep on the other side of the line. His trembling fingers managed to dial 911, and for a fraction of a second, there was a silence that froze his blood. Immediately, he heard the ring, and a female voice answered:

"Nine one one, what is your emergency?"

"Hi, it's Lucas, I was kidnapped by a psycho, and I don't know where I am! Please come quickly!" That's what he meant to say, but instead, his lips let out a series of incomprehensible babble.

“I’m sorry, can you repeat that?” The woman asked in a tone so calm it was frustrating.

“I-I’m Lucas,” he managed to say, tears flowing from his eyes. “I was kidnapped, and, and.... I’m... please, you have to help me...”

“Do you know where you are now, Lucas?” she asked without changing her tone.

“No!” He shouted as he wiped his face with his forearm, hearing someone else’s voice made him feel better.

“Can you peek through a window?”

He glanced at the wall in front of him until he found his own reflection staring back in a glass a few meters away from him.

“There’s a fence outside, but that’s all I can see. It’s very dark.” Once he said those words, he realized the light would go off at any moment.

“Do not worry, Lucas, just stay with me as long as you can, okay?”

Was she crazy? He couldn’t do such a thing. At that moment, he was using all his willpower not to drop the phone and run to the other side of the hallway. He wanted to say he was fine, that he would stay with her for as long as necessary but couldn’t.

“Lucas? Are you still there?”

He opened his mouth to answer but was interrupted by a click. Next thing he knew, he was wrapped in a cloak of darkness.

CHAPTER 9

Lucas screamed. The burst of dread ran through the house, shaking the walls. The wind responded with a roar from outside. He imagined himself running at full speed to the door, or throwing himself out from the second floor's window. Anything was better than being there. However, his legs did not respond, and his hands clutched the plastic tightly against his ear; if he let go, he would lose his only opportunity to escape, the only person willing to help him in that moment of crisis.

"Lucas?" Asked the lady on the other side of the line, her voice now showed a tinge of concern; although, he could tell that she was trying to maintain her composure. "Lucas, are you ok? Are you still there?"

"Please…"

"Tell me what's going on."

Another click made him jump, and the sudden flash of light forced him to close his eyes. He blinked several times as his vision adjusted to the brightness again.

"You have to come," Lucas begged. "They want to kill me!"

It was horrible to hear himself say those words because they gave weight to what was happening; they grounded him in reality. This was not a nightmare; his mother was not there to hug him and tell him that it was only a dream, nor was his father there to calm him and assure him that everything would be fine, that there were no monsters under the bed or ghosts in the closet. This was real. He was in real danger, and the monsters existed; only they were not like in the movies, they were disguised in human skin.

"Who wants to hurt you, sweetheart?"

"The Andersons," he replied.

"Anderson..." she repeated. "How old are you?"

He didn't understand the sudden change of subject, but he answered anyway:

"Eleven."

"Let me tell you that you are a very brave young man, and very intelligent. You will be fine, do you hear me?"

"Yes," he said, he could hear her, but he couldn't believe her.

"Is there any place where you can hide?"

"Yes, I think so."

"Well, listen, what you're going to do is..."

The lamp died again, and Lucas let out a scream.

"No, no, no, no, no, no, this is a nightmare."

"You'll be fine," she reassured him.

"This is not happening; this is a nightmare..." Lucas repeated. "This is not happening... this is a nightmare..."

He recited the mantra again and again with the hope that, sooner or later, he would end up believing it. The light returned as unexpectedly as it had gone. He opened his eyes. Everything looked blurry as if he had just gotten up. A shadow stood in front of him; huge like a tower, holding something long that ended with a metal edge in his hand. It was Martin carrying a shovel.

He blinked several times as he prayed for it to be only a part of his imagination, but instead of disappearing, the horror became clearer.

"What's all the screaming about?" Martin roared, the muscles in his arms were rigid as rocks. "And what are you doing out of your room, you piece of shit...?" He paused in the middle of the sentence as his wild eyes stuck on the phone. "What the fuck...? Were you calling someone?"

A chill ran down Lucas's spine, and he felt as if the ground had collapsed. He put the phone back in place without looking away from Martin; the madman's eyes seemed about to come out of his skull, the red veins around his pupils about to explode. Martin took a step toward him. Lucas mumbled, instinctively taking one back.

"This is going to be fun," Martin said, a grotesque grin spreading from ear to ear, revealing a row of rotting teeth.

The giant threw himself at Lucas with his shovel in the air. An adrenaline rush swept Lucas out of his trance. The lamp went out. He stepped back and fell backward on the wooden floor. The wind shook right in front of his nose accompanied by a grunt. The shovel had been inches away from his face.

Lucas turned and crawled as fast as he could, without seeing where he was going. His hand reached a pillar of wood. It was the leg of one of the little tables in the hallway. He shook it and rolled to his left.

"There you are, you little shit!" Martin yelled and slammed the shovel into something that burst into a thousand pieces.

The fragments of what must have been a vase rained over Lucas's legs as he crawled away.

"Son of a bitch!" Martin shouted. "Look what you made me do!"

Lucas put a knee on his chest and got back up. He ran towards the intersection of the other corridor. At last, he was able to see the world around him, but it wouldn't last for long. He looked at the switch on the wall for an eternal few seconds. He knew what he had to do, but he was reluctant; there must be another way to outwit this maniac.

"I see you," whispered Martin behind him.

Lucas lowered the switch and jumped towards the balcony that served as a corridor, returning where he had come without looking back. His hand slid down the railing as he ran. He looked down and was tempted to jump outside, but his common sense guided him to the end of the hall.

Martin's footsteps echoed like drums behind him. Lucas didn't dare to look over his shoulder, convinced that he would die if he did. He finally reached the door that led to the stairs and pushed it open. As soon as his foot touched the first step, the cold metal of the shovel struck his back. The next thing he knew he was flying, his face heading directly for the steps.

CHAPTER 10

Lucas flew down the stairs. His legs sought support in the air as his arms rose instinctively to cover his face. First, his elbows met the edge of the steps, then his side and the rest of his body, which rolled the rest of the way, finally crashing head-on against the ground.

His whole body screamed in agony. Threads of tears, snot, and blood slid from his face. He crawled a few inches before trying to sit up, but he felt like he was carrying a hundred pounds on his back. His arms trembled.

Martin's huge foot rested on him, crushing him with its weight. A pang of pain ran through his spine and ribs. Lucas let out a sharp, puppy-like scream.

"Shut up, you pussy!" Martin yelled. "Can't you take a little rough play?"

The giant grabbed Lucas by the shoulder and turned him over. He clasped his hand in the collar of the boy's shirt. Lucas's limbs hung like rubber as Martin lifted him. A faint glow, barely visible, reflected on the man's hip.

Lucas focused all his energy on moving his right hand, tangling his fingers in the keys that Martin carried on his belt, and pulled with what little strength he had left, tearing the fabric of Martin's pants. Lucas's small hand seized the keys. He quickly moved them to form a fist, with a key coming out between each finger.

"What the fuck do you think you're doing?" Martin asked.

Lucas waited until he was face to face with Martin. He clenched his fist, feeling the metal embedded in his delicate palm and struck the man with all his might as the keys sank into Martin's cheek. The big man let out a scream and dropped Lucas.

The boy fell on his back and shrieked in pain. Meanwhile, Martin wiped the blood off his face.

"Son of a bitch!" He shouted. "I'm gonna kill you for that! You hear me!"

Lucas backed away crawling, he pushed himself up with both hands and ran to the front door. He hurriedly fitted the first key he found. It slipped into the hole tightly. He turned and heard a click, mixed with Martin's grunts. Frantically, Lucas turned the knob and pushed the double doors wide open.

Lucas wanted to run, but his legs didn't respond. In front of him, wooden steps led down to a courtyard full of trees and bushes, and after that, nothing. Complete darkness.

There wasn't a single light source outside. There were no signs of a streetlamp or any road. It was as if they were in the middle of nowhere. Trapped in limbo, where only the house existed, surrounded by the same blackness from which the universe was made.

Lucas didn't realize he was shaking. His eyes, wide open, could not escape the immense, menacing darkness. At that moment, he forgot everything that had happened. The only thing he was conscious of was a duality in his mind—two voices screaming contradictions. One begged him to escape, to throw himself into the night and receive its embrace. The other demanded that he close the doors and back away as far as possible. He didn't know which one to listen to. Both were born out of absolute terror.

Lucas barely felt the giant hands that grabbed and carried him effortlessly inside. The doors closed, and he could not help feeling immense gratitude, although for some reason he knew he should be terrified.

Soon, he realized his mistake. He had hesitated, and now Martin was dragging him back to the house, his distorted smile matching the blood on his face.

Lucas screamed and kicked uselessly as Martin carried him to a worn wooden door with a metal bolt. Martin kicked it open. A putrid scent struck Lucas face. It was a mixture of moisture, rotten wood, and metal. Stairs went down as far as his eye could see.

The boy screamed harder and began to punch his kidnapper, who didn't seem to be affected in the slightest.

"Let me go! Please! I won't tell anyone, please!" Lucas screamed.

"Shut up, you puss. I told you to behave, but you didn't listen, so now I'm gonna have to punish you."

"You're lying!" Lucas's face was red like a tomato and his eyes soaked with tears. "You were going to hurt me anyway!"

Martin's voice was chilling. "Maybe you're right." The big man was having a hard time descending the steps while holding the hysterical child. "I would've come up with any excuse sooner or later just to see you cry like the little baby you are. If you had listened, right now you would be sleeping in your room, and I would be watching TV. But no, you decided to be a little pain in the ass. You don't have anyone else to blame but yourself."

Lucas dug his nails into Martin's skin. He had guessed his captor's intentions the moment they crossed the threshold and started to descend. Martin was going to lock him up and leave him abandoned in a dirty basement where who knew what might be lurking around.

Lucas pushed himself up trying to bite Martin's ear, but the man lifted his chin to avoid it. As they reached the last step, Lucas noticed that the only source of light came from the entrance, leaving the stairs and the gray mold-covered walls barely visible.

Martin threw Lucas into an invisible corner as if he were a sack of dirty clothes. The boy crashed into a puddle of stagnant water. The hard ground scraped his elbows, which glowed red. Lucas tried to sit up, but his wet hands slid off the wall as he tried to lean on it.

"Stay right there," Martin ordered. "If by the time I'm back, you moved even an inch, your death will be slow and painful."

"No, please!" Lucas begged, crawling toward the stairs. "I'll be good! I promise! Please don't lock me in here!"

"There's nothing to negotiate, kid," Martin said as he climbed the creaking steps.

"No! Don't leave! Don't leave me alone, please!"

"I won't be long." Martin looked over his shoulder and grinned. "I'm just going to get my favorite toy. You deserve something different from the others."

Martin reached the top, and a halo of light surrounded his silhouette. He put his hand on the bolt and started to close it.

"No! No! Turn on the light! Please! TURN ON THE LIGHT!"

The door closed and everything ceased to exist.

CHAPTER 11

Lucas screamed as hard as he could until his throat started to burn and his chest hurt with every breath. Finally, after an eternity of uncertainty, his eyes began to adjust. Gray figures took shape around him; a wall, a pillar. Everything became more clear with each blink.

His nose, on the other hand, could not adapt to the putrid scent that enveloped him. The smell was so intense it made him dizzy. Lucas tried to hold his breath, but every so often he was forced to take a deep breath, which only made matters worse. In the distance, an incessant drip echoed. With tremendous effort, he found the strength to get back on his feet.

Just a few feet in front of him, there was a black figure lying on the ground. From a distance, it looked like a statue, but as he approached, he realized that it was something else. Not quite sure what, he crouched to take a better look at it.

A few seconds passed before he could see what lay in front of him. It was a person, small, in a fetal position, looking straight at the wall. Lucas fell back, almost screaming, but the pain in his throat contained the cry, giving him a fit of cough instead.

Lucas coughed until his eyes filled with tears. He was sure that whoever was in front of him was a boy, younger than him, wearing a t-shirt and shorts; he was also skinny, very skinny. The nauseating smell was coming from the child.

He's sleeping. He must be sleeping, he thought, trying to calm himself. He stretched out his leg and gave the boy a little kick with the tip of his foot. The boy didn't flinch.

"Hey," Lucas whispered. "Wake up. We have to get out of here."

Lucas kicked him again, a little tougher this time; still no reply. He knelt on the damp floor and put a hand on the boy's shoulder. It was cold and hard; his t-shirt was covered with a viscous liquid, and the stench was unbearable.

Lucas turned the boy around, and a pale face with empty sockets stared back at him. What was left of the boy's skin stretched over his bones like loose clothing, his mouth open and larvae crawling between his teeth.

All of Lucas's muscles were instantly paralyzed, and he was overcome with vertigo. He had never seen a dead person in real life—only in movies, and no matter how realistic the makeup or the dolls were, he could always tell it was not a real person.

This was totally different. It was somebody like him, a boy who used to play with his friends in the park, who had hopes and fears and dreams of the future, and who was now being eaten by worms.

Lucas stood up and ran wildly away from the dead boy with his hands up in the air until he hit the wall. He was drenched with water to his knees. The mixture of horror and wet cold made him shudder. Unsure of what he was doing or where he was headed, Lucas made his way deeper into the basement, trying to put as much distance as possible between himself and the corpse.

With his heart hammering in his throat, he guided himself by sliding his fingers against the wall, terrified that the boy's decomposed face would leap at him out of the dark.

Instead, he hit something that made him jump. A humanoid figure stood in front of him, threatening. Lucas went around it before it could do anything to him and stumbled across another specter. His pace quickened, his arms outstretched, pushing away everything in his path.

"Get away from me!" he shouted, tears streaming down his cheeks.

Finally, he reached one of the corners and squatted without looking away from his pursuers. It was then he noticed something odd about them—they weren't moving. There were rows of what appeared to be people in different positions, all inert. More corpses? He gagged at the thought. There was no way he could bear to see another body.

More than anything, Lucas wanted to close his eyes, but he blinked several times, doing his best to focus on the ghosts. Most of them were pale, contrasting with the dark walls. Some seemed to have garments while others did not. They were all arranged in strange positions.

The answer came to him like lightning. They were mannequins.

Lucas took a puff of rotting air and exhaled in tears. He slid down the wall until his knees reached his chest, sobbing harder than ever. His mother, his father; how worried they would be when they realized he wasn't home, how much they would suffer when they discovered that he had died in the cold basement of a psychopath—if they ever found out. He didn't know what was worse, having to discover their son's terrible fate or having to live in uncertainty, always waiting for an answer that would never come.

That was what the family of that dead boy must've been going through. He felt sorry for him, for them, for all the victims the Andersons had taken. Lucas tried to pray, as his mother had told him to do whenever he was afraid, but he knew that it would not do any good. Praying would not revive the child or return him to his family. God had no mercy on him, so why would He have it for Lucas?

Suddenly, a yellow light blinded him. He covered his face with his forearm as he tried to recover his vision. A bulb swayed from the ceiling. The wooden stairs creaked to the rhythm of footsteps.

Martin had returned to finish what he started.

CHAPTER 12

Lucas hid behind one of the boxes in front of him, surrounded by a dozen dead-eyed mannequins. He tried to make himself as small as possible in the space he had. He was sure whoever was coming down the stairs had not heard him, but it was only a matter of time before they found him.

The mannequins projected long, deformed shadows that danced on the walls. The footsteps became more prominent every second until they reached their inevitable end in the puddle at the foot of the stairs. Lucas glanced between the mannequins, expecting to see the seven-foot-tall giant with a rusty ax in his hands. Instead, he saw a pale woman with long black hair slide down into the basement, with one hand on her chest and the other one held high as if she were waltzing.

Now that he saw Bella without makeup, he realized how old she was as if twenty years of life had suddenly fallen upon her. Her eyes were on top of two black bags, the wrinkles on her forehead imitating the curves of the ocean.

The woman approached the nearest mannequin, a gentleman in a button-down shirt and dress pants. She extended her hands to him as an invitation.

"Shall we dance?"

Without waiting for an answer, she grabbed her plastic companion and began to dance with him, taking him from one side to the other in delicate strides to the rhythm of music that only she could hear.

"Isn't it wonderful, my dear?" Bella asked the mannequin, her eyes shining as if she was in front of a blue prince. "Promise me we'll be together forever." The mannequin did not respond. "Tonight I'm the happiest woman in the world. I'm lucky to have a man like you."

Lucas remembered the photographs of the Anderson's wedding and, without any explanation, felt great pity for the woman. However, the feeling did not last long, considering the fact that a few feet from her was the decomposing body of a child who he was sure wasn't hers.

Lucas looked at the stairs, uncertain whether or not he should take the risk. Meanwhile, Bella lowered her hand to the crotch of his companion with a mischievous look.

"Are you armed or just happy to see me? Whatever the answer, I like it."

Without warning, Bella's grin twisted into a grimace. Her face dropped, tears falling from her eyes. She rested her head on the mannequin's chest as she sobbed.

Lucas had to seize the opportunity. He circled the mannequins around him silently, sliding between them with his head down, looking at Bella to make sure she didn't see him. He was tempted to run, but he resisted the urge.

Once out of the plastic jungle, he found himself in a predicament. The whole basement was flooded. Even if he strolled, his footsteps would be heard. He looked up. Bella's face was still buried in the mannequin's chest. Lucas wondered how far he could go if he ran, whether she would catch him first or whether he would have a chance to reach the door.

He glanced around the room in search of some distraction, a rock he could throw or something. Anything would do. He thought about knocking down the mannequins, but that would only reveal his location before he even had a chance to run. He was starting to give up when his gaze settled on the wall beside him. A white switch stood on the wall.

It made sense to have two light switches in the basement: one right at the entrance and the other one inside. After all, no one wanted to be trapped in the dark.

Lucas paused. The thought of being swallowed again by darkness made his heart race at a thousand beats per second. But this was his only chance; if he didn't face his fear, then he would end up like that boy on the floor.

He put his hand on the switch and lowered it. Water splashed beneath his feet as he ran, full speed, his eyes fixed on where the stairs were supposed to be, desperately trying not to think about the horrors hiding all around him.

He could feel Bella's gaze like a sharp knife on the back of his neck as his hand reached the wooden railing. He used it to pull himself up, skipping as many steps as he could. Out of the corner of his eye, he saw a white figure rushing toward him, her face covered by long greasy hair.

"What are you doing here?! Don't run, you son of a bitch!"

Lucas reached for the door handle just as he felt cold, bony fingers wrap around his ankle and pull him back. Lucas' hand tightened on the handle. He let out a scream as he kicked, trying to push himself forward.

He dared a glance over his shoulder. Bella's eyes were bloodshot, swollen. Her nose was wrinkled like the rest of her face in fury. Lucas tried to kick her, but his foot twisted in all directions. With his free hand, he groped for the switch on the side of the door. He closed his eyes and pulled it up.

The bulb that hung right next to them flashed with blinding yellow light. Bella screamed, her fingers loosened, and Lucas slipped from her grasp. He pushed against the door with all his might, opening it, and then slammed it shut behind him. On one side hung a chain that worked as a lock. Bella knocked on the door, hysterical, while Lucas, leaning his weight against the door, put the chain on the handle.

"Let me out, you fucking brat! Let me out!"

Lucas stepped back panting, his shirt soaked with cold sweat. Ignoring Bella's insults, he turned and headed for the main entrance.

Once there, he paused to stare at the double doors that stood defiantly in front of him. He had survived a few falls, one down the stairs and another in the basement. There were definitely worse things than the dark. That was clear to him now, and it was something he would remember for the rest of his life—but how long would that be? Lucas shook off those thoughts. The boy in the basement, the tub full of blood in the bathroom, he refused to end up like that. With a last deep breath, he put his hand on the doorknob.

However, he heard heavy footsteps coming from the other side of the door. Lucas stepped back; he knew who it was. The curtains that covered the windows were filled with a huge shadow that shifted from side to side, moving closer and closer to the door.

Without hesitation, Lucas raced to the opposite side of the lobby, running up the stairs and entering another of the endless corridors in this vast house of terror. Almost without thinking, he got inside one of the rooms, one he hadn't been in before.

He closed the door behind him as he entered, unaware that someone was watching him from a corner of the room.

CHAPTER 13

Lucas heard a creak behind him. He jumped and looked back. In one corner of the room lay a king-sized bed, and wrapped around the stained sheets was the old woman he'd met earlier. On the side of the bed sat the wheelchair in which she had been sitting a few hours earlier.

"Oh." Lucas sighed with relief. "It's you!" She raised her hand inches from his chest as if to greet him. "Thank you for what you did before, for covering me, I mean."

The woman smiled wanly. Lucas walked scanned the room as he walked over to the old woman. Right in front of the bed was a hairdresser with a broken mirror; its wood looked discolored and rotten, probably termites. The room seemed small to be an adult's, not to mention that the walls were painted light blue.

"Is this where you sleep?" Lucas asked. She nodded, the smile fading from her face. Lucas had so many questions to ask, but not all of them could be answered with yes or no. Communicating with her was going to be a challenge. Lucas liked that. "Do you have a pen and paper?"

The lady nodded again. Her gaunt hand reached up and, with her index finger, she pointed to the hairdresser. Lucas obeyed, half expecting to find makeup combs and cases on the surface, but there was only a thick layer of dust. He opened the first drawer and saw a pile of newspaper articles piled on top of each other as if they had been thrown in at random. What struck him was that the clippings were from different newspapers and from several dates.

There were square cutouts; the small ones, which were at the top, displayed names. Lucas picked up one that caught his eye. It had a photo of a smiling boy about eight years old.

Adrian Torres

You did not deserve to leave the way you did. You were a victim of human cruelty and malice. The only consolation I have left is to know that you are at peace now. The whole family prays for you and misses you. You will be remembered dearly. I will see you in the afterlife, my love.

May you rest in peace, my baby, and may God forgive me for not being there when you needed me most.

Lucas dropped the paper. It was an obituary, and it was recent. He didn't have to be a genius to imagine that it was one of the Anderson's victims. He was sure it was not the boy in the basement, though. The one in the picture looked younger, and the obituary would not be in the newspaper if the family didn't know his whereabouts. A shiver ran down his spine as tears flooded his eyes.

He reached in the drawer, picked the clipping up again, and held it up to the old woman.

"They did this, didn't they?" Lucas asked.

The old woman nodded somberly. Lucas wanted to say something, but he was not sure what. All of this was a nightmare. He just wanted to get out of there, to see his family again. But that seemed like an increasingly impossible dream.

He continued rifling through the clippings without saying anything more. Another story caught his attention, this one larger than the last, with the photograph of a house wreathed in flames. He could not look away. The title was just as captivating.

<u>Infant dies in a tragic accident</u>

Local sources reported that around 3:30 am today, residents alerted authorities to a fire on Main Avenue. The property belonged to the

Anderson family. Martin Anderson and his wife Isabella Anderson managed to escape with their eldest son just in time; however, their youngest daughter, barely three months old, perished in the fire.

Mr. Anderson said that the flames consumed the child's room in a matter of seconds and spread through the house at an alarming rate. According to the testimonies, Mrs. Anderson had left the water heater on while preparing dinner. By the time the smoke reached the first floor, it was too late.

The story went on, but Lucas refused to continue reading. Another article stood out from the others in the back of the cabinet.

Family loses custody of surviving child

Mr. Martin Anderson and Mrs. Isabella Anderson, a middle-aged couple who lost their youngest daughter, Eva, in a fire two weeks ago, have lost custody of their surviving child at the early age of three. The child will remain in charge of the state due to allegations of child abuse and neglect. He will be assigned to an orphanage until a family is found that is willing to adopt him. Due to his young age, he should have no memory of the horrors he has had to endure

Enough! He didn't have to read anymore. However, he couldn't deny that things were starting to make sense, in some twisted way. The Andersons had lost their daughter in a fire and then custody of their other child. They went crazy and now kidnapped any kid they found to make them part of the family. That also explained why the room he woke up in looked like a girl's room.

He reached in and pushed aside the rest of the papers. There was a photograph between them. It was a gray stain wrapped in a black background; it did not seem to have shape. On the back, the words "*Forgive me, Eva*" were written in delicate handwriting. It took a couple of seconds for Lucas to realize that it was one of those pictures taken of babies while they are in their mother's womb. Lucas turned to the lady.

"It wasn't their fault, but they are responsible for the deaths of the other children, the ones they brought here."

The old woman's face remained blank. Lucas waited for an answer that never came. He remembered what he had to do and returned to his task. Finally, his fingers felt the plastic of a pen, and he took it out. He snatched a piece out of one of the clippings, approached the woman who was staring at him from the bed, and put the paper and pen on her lap.

"What is your name?"

She wrote, her fingers shaking with each letter, all of her attention focused on the paper. Finally, she set the pen aside and handed him the paper with a scribble barely readable.

"Ta ... Tania?" he asked, unsure.

Tania nodded. At last Lucas could put a name on the face of the woman who had saved him.

"You're not like them… why are you with them? I mean, I know he's your son, and he's taking care of you, but I don't see why. I think you'd be better off somewhere else."

Tania picked up the pen again, this time she wrote two words: "Husband, died." Lucas dodged her gaze as he saw the old woman's watery eyes.

"Oh, then, I guess you had no choice." Lucas opened his mouth and closed it again, afraid to ask the question he really wanted to ask. "Did any of the other children come out alive?" Tania shook her head from side to side. "There has to be something I can do."

Instead of writing, Tania pointed to the window. Lucas understood what she meant. He had to leave as soon as possible, but it was not an easy task. He couldn't take the risk without knowing where his pursuers were.

Having to go around every corner full of uncertainty and doubt, fearing that every moment that passed could be the last. It was something he had never felt in his life and was keeping him from thinking clearly.

“Thanks for everything,” Lucas finally said.

He set off to look out the window to see if it was safe to go to the main door, but Tania grabbed him by the arm before he finished turning around. She pointed to the hairdresser as if to ask for something.

“You want something else from there?”

Tania nodded. He checked through all the drawers this time. He pulled out the newspapers, which were next to several objects that did not seem to have any relation between each other, from scissors and tape to a box of cigarettes and a lighter. Luke patiently lifted each of the objects to see what she wanted. She chose two things: the cigarette and the lighter.

Lucas hesitated for a second. He wasn’t sure that a woman her age should be smoking, but he owed her his life, so he felt compelled to give them to her. She lit the cigarette expertly, despite the instability of her hands. She took a long breath and exhaled the smoke, turning her head to the other side so that Lucas wouldn’t breathe it in. Suddenly, the woman’s gaze seemed to change, instead of the coarse grimace, she looked relieved, as relaxed as if she was on a tropical beach. Lucas appreciated that she had a moment of peace.

"Is there anything else you need?" Lucas asked as he fumbled in his pockets.

He only pulled out a bit of lint, a few coins, and the bottle of sleeping pills, the one he'd taken from the bathroom. He'd completely forgotten he still had it. The old woman's eyes widened, and she pointed to the flask.

"Do you want the pills?" Lucas asked doubtfully. "Well, I suppose if you want to sleep, they are good. They are the same ones my mom uses."

With a shrug, he handed the bottle to the old woman, who shook it between her fingers. She opened it; several pills fell on the sheet. She grabbed them all again with the other hand and emptied the bottle into her palm. There were a lot.

"Wow… hey, you grabbed too many..."

Before he could complete the sentence, the old woman took all the pills into her mouth and swallowed them in one gulp. Lucas jumped over and grabbed both of her hands. But his efforts were in vain; it was already too late.

"No! What are you doing? You can't swallow them all!"

Tania put her hands on Lucas's wrists and gently pushed them away. Her moist eyes shone with a comforting look. Lucas felt impotent. He could have forced her to spit them out, perhaps sticking his fingers in her throat, but Tania's gaze told him that this was what she wanted. All she wanted was peace, and this was her way of getting it.

"No, please..." Lucas begged, knowing it was useless.

His eyes grew wet. The old woman put a finger to her lips, imploring him to remain silent. Until then, Lucas had completely forgotten about Martin and Bella; they had passed into the background for the first time all night.

Tania's eyes began to close, and Lucas knew she was stepping into an eternal dream, one that she had craved for who knew how long.

Lucas wiped his tears; his new friend looked placid, calm, at peace with herself. A slight curve appeared on her lips giving the impression of a smile. Maybe it was.

He had no idea how long he stood there, watching Tania. He did not care either. He could have stayed the rest of the night without moving if something unusual had not caught his attention.

From the window, flickering lights peered through the curtains; the colors were intense red and blue. He rushed toward the window as soon as he saw it. Outside, right in front of the iron fence, a police car was parked. While he could not read the letters on the side of the vehicle, the colors were unmistakable.

The call he made before had worked. He had given up on the idea of waiting for help, that someone would come to rescue him at any moment, but now there was a real possibility of getting out of there and into the hands of someone who would keep him safe.

He headed back to the bed with the intention of saying goodbye. However, at that precise moment, the lights throughout the house went out, and the room turned dim. He could feel the pressure on his chest, a familiar fear, only this time he did not feel the urge to scream. He took a long breath and groped in the dark until he found the unmistakable shape of the lighter.

He set it on fire, and, with no more time to lose, went to the door in search of his freedom.

CHAPTER 14

Lucas left the room with the lighter in his hand, the orange light projecting irregular shadows around him. He could hardly see what was in front of him. He reached the stairs, turned off the lighter to avoid being seen, and leaned down.

The main entrance door was wide open. There seemed to be no one on the other side.

"Hello?" Called a voice he'd never heard before. It came from inside the house. "The door was open! If there is anyone here, please respond, it's the police!"

Lucas opened his mouth until his jaw reached his chest, inhaled as much air as he could, his throat ready to scream. Suddenly a flash of light caught his attention, causing him to stifle his cry for help. It was Bella, with a flashlight in her hand, stalking, combing the area. He couldn't let her know where he was.

"Is anyone here?" insisted the policeman.

Bella, her face contorted with anger and frustration, turned and went to the source of the voice. Lucas hesitated for a few seconds and then decided to climb down the stairs.

Carefully, he reached the bottom without making the slightest noise. Once again on the first floor, he found himself facing the entrance. In the distance, he could see the blinking lights of the police car. The red and blue flashes invited him to escape. And for a second, Lucas almost fell into temptation.

However, things are not always that easy. It was a lesson he had learned, along with many others, throughout the night. The road to the police car was so dark he could barely make out the shape of it. Even if he ran, he didn't know what he would find on the way. He pictured Martin jumping out of the bushes with a chainsaw in his hands, trying to cut him in half. After all, Lucas never knew if Martin got inside the house after seeing his shadow outside the window. So, he might still be out there, waiting for the best time to strike.

On the other hand, the officer was inside the house, and Bella was prowling in the dark. If he went looking for the officer, he risked her catching him first. What was the right path? What would lead him to safety? He didn't know. But if he had to choose between bumping into

Bella or Martin, he would definitely pick Bella. Besides, even if he got to the car safely, it was no use since there was no one inside. He was closer to the driver than to the car anyway.

Lucas made his decision and entered the confines of that huge, but suffocating house.

He opened the double doors leading to the hallways. He lit the lighter, though the place was already disorienting with all the lamps on; now it was a real maze. On several occasions he had to stop and think where he was going, trying to remember as much as possible of his previous journey.

The orange light from the lighter reflected off the portraits of the Anderson family around him, which gave him a clearer idea of where he was. The only way left was the one that led to the dining room.

"Huh?"

Bella's voice made his heart stop for a second as a white beam of light streamed down the hall from the kitchen. Lucas extinguished the lighter off immediately.

"Is anyone there?" Bella whispered, almost as if she didn't want to be heard.

He heard the steps approaching and saw the circle of light drawn on the wall grow larger. Lucas stepped back slowly. The pale figure of the woman peered down the hall.

"It's the police!" Shouted the officer from somewhere unknown.

Lucas looked over his shoulder trying to find the source of the voice. At some point, Lucas must have taken a different corridor from which the officer was going.

He looked back, and there was Bella, her deformed face flashing a malicious smile, her black hair stuck to her forehead. Lucas ran back into the living room. He had nothing to lose now.

"Help! Please!" He yelled as he moved through the dark corridors, guided by the frantic light from Bella's lantern behind him.

He pushed the double doors with all the weight of his body, which crashed against the walls in a clatter. In the middle of the hall, right in front of the television and with the body facing him, a black figure stood. He carried what appeared to be a pistol with both hands. A bright police badge hung on his chest. Lucas thanked the universe for getting there.

"Please" he implored, panting. "You have to help me; they're chasing me. They want to kill me!"

"Calm down, champ," said the officer. Up close, Lucas could see his well-combed black hair and blue eyes. "One word at the time. Who is chasing you?"

"Her!" Lucas turned and pointed behind him.

To his surprise, no one was there.

"Everything will be all right," said the officer. "Come with me, and you can explain everything to me on the way."

Lucas nodded, filled with hope that he would soon escape this torment. The officer put the pistol back in his belt and held out his hand to him. Lucas raised his.

Just then, a deafening roar shook everything. In a flicker, the officer's head turned into an explosion of blood, gunpowder, and bits of brain that scattered in all directions. One of his blue eyes rolled across the floor between pieces of skull. The rest of his body remained standing for two endless seconds; half his head turned into a red mass that spilled over on all sides until he finally fell to the floor like a rag doll.

Lucas' legs loosened and failed as he stumbled back. He watched with his mouth open as Martin came out of the shadows with a shotgun in both hands, threads of smoke coming out of its metallic mouth. Martin gave a howl of emotion.

"So much fun!" Lucas didn't know how to react; he felt the adrenaline rush through his body. "Don't worry, son; I'll play with you too in a bit. But first I want you to explain to me what you're doing out here. Didn't I tell you to stay in the basement? I just wanted to show you my favorite toy" He put the shotgun up and looked at it as if it were a trophy. "Beautiful, isn't it?"

CHAPTER 15

"Answer me when I speak to you."

Lucas stayed mute with his gaze now fixed on the pool of blood that shrouded his feet. What was in front of him was disgusting, but he still could not take his eyes off the policeman, or rather, what was left of him. The lamps in the corridor came to life; the light had returned just in time so that he could appreciate the spectacle in greater detail.

"You like what you see, don't you?" Martin laughed. "Of course you do; it's amazing." Martin's voice sounded distant as if he was speaking from another room. Lucas' ears were trying to recover from a gunshot fired mere inches from him, after all. "I remember I used to play cat and mouse with my old man a long time ago." The seven-foot-tall man put one knee on the floor and brought his face to Lucas. "It's very simple, you see, it's like hide and seek, only you cannot stay hidden in one place for too long because, if I catch you, it's game over. The difference is that he used to punish me in other ways. I'll use my little toy. My piece of advice for you is to run."

Obediently, Lucas got to his feet and ran in the opposite direction. He returned to the hallways. He could feel Martin's enormous feet on his heels, and that was part of his plan. He would run around the kitchen and dining room to the other door leading to the hall. In other words, he would try to make a full circle around the house and back to the main lobby. Once there, he would hurl himself toward the exit, no longer caring if he had to run blindly through the forest if that meant getting away from that maniac. He didn't want to end up like the cop. Watching him, so closely, he realized how fragile the human body was. One moment you are a conscious person, alive and well, and the next, nothing more than a sack of bones and blood.

He moved through the kitchen at full speed, with the smell of alcohol and grime behind him. He crossed the dining room until finally reaching the hallway that led to the lobby again. His feet guided him back to where he came from. And there it was, the elusive exit, waiting for him.

Lucas ran with his hand up as if he was trying to touch the freedom with his fingers. But just as he reached the threshold, the door slammed shut in front of him. He could feel the fresh air slipping out of his grasp.

And he saw it, at the side of the door, the pale spectrum of black hair.

"Where do you think you're going, sweetie?" Bella asked mockingly. "You're not going to leave mommy alone, are you?"

"You're not my mother," Lucas barked, clenching his fists.

"Excuse me?"

"Get out of the way!"

Bella put her hand to her breast with feigned indignation.

"How dare you speak to your mother like that, you little brat?"

Martin's footsteps grew louder.

"I don't have time!" Lucas yelled. "Get out of the way!"

Bella came up to him with her hands up, as if she was going to carry him; her long, claw-like nails grew closer to him. It was then that he realized that they were going directly to his neck.

"I will teach you to respect your elders."

Bella lunged at him. Lucas stepped back. Behind him, Martin appeared with the shotgun held high pointing straight at the back of his head.

"There you are!" Martin shouted.

In an instant, Lucas lunged to the side landing on his elbows and knees. Martin pulled the trigger.

The shot was deafening. Lucas watched in horror as a red hole appeared in Bella's white blouse, covering almost her entire torso. The wood beneath her feet splashed red.

Martin gasped, his shotgun still high, his wife staggering before her legs failed and she fell on her back.

"I-Isabella..."

The giant stepped erratically towards his wife. The light had gone out of her eyes. Martin fell to his knees, wrapped his arms around her, and let out a spine-chilling scream, a mixture of soul-piercing pain and hatred.

Lucas seized his opportunity and fled.

CHAPTER 16

"Come here, you little fucker!"

The words shook the house, and Lucas knew he was going to die. He ran down the aisles looking for a place to hide, knowing it was useless. Wherever he went, Martin would find him and blow his brains out as he had done to that cop. He could still see the red, pink, and white mixture of tissue exploding through the air. He bit his lip to hold back the tears, his legs carrying him without direction.

"You can't hide forever!"

The scream was close. Lucas picked up the pace. He crossed to the dining room, and his eyes took in all the information they could. No place to hide except the table. Better than nothing.

He threw himself on the floor and crawled under the table, moving the chairs to the side to get in. The moment his body was covered entirely; he knew he had made a big mistake.

Large black boots peered out the door, stained with blood, leaving red marks on the wooden floor. Lucas felt his heart about to burst open from his chest. All Martin had to do was crouch to find him. The boots crossed the dining room, each step shaking the floor, and then they returned. Just as they reached the door, Martin stopped and turned. The soles of his boots looked directly at Lucas. They seemed to smirk at him. He'd been spotted.

Lucas jumped. His head hit the tabletop, knocking over everything on top. The glass shattered on the floor as Lucas crawled out as fast as he could.

"Son of a bitch!" yelled Martin in a voice so guttural that it didn't sound like it had come from a human being.

A blast behind him made him stop; he saw over his shoulder that Martin had fired at the table; thousands of splinters along with pieces of wood and pottery flew through the air. If Lucas had taken a fraction of a second more to get out, he would've been blown into a thousand pieces.

He entered the kitchen and was driven to the cabinet that held the cleaning products. He fumbled and quickly found the huge white bottle of bleach in the back. He grabbed the handle and pulled it out of the way, knocking over everything in between.

Don't touch that, Lucas! You'll go blind!

"Better blind than dead." He whispered to himself.

He turned and headed for the exit that led back to the hallway as Martin entered the room, the shotgun up. Another blast shook the room, this one stronger than the previous one; Lucas could see the cloud of death spitting out of the gun. The cabinet exploded behind him. He ran down the hall to the living room. His ears began to ache; he heard Martin's distant voice cursing as if he were on the other side of a cave.

Lucas carried the heavy bottle of bleach with both hands. He spotted the door at the end of the hallway and rammed into it with his shoulder, using all of his weight. It flew open, and Lucas had to sway to keep his balance. He saw the stairs and started up at full speed.

A third roar behind him made him bow his head and drop the bleach bottle, which rolled down the stairs. The lid ended up on one of the steps, and Lucas watched with horror as the liquid spilled with the bottle rolling all the way to the floor.

He came down with his hand on the railing. He picked up the bottle and noticed that it weighed much less than before.

"No!" he cried, "No, no, no."

He looked up and saw the black mouth of the shotgun, fixed on him. Martin was smiling from ear to ear, his face twisted in a grimace of pleasure and hatred. Lucas closed his eyes, and Martin pulled the trigger.

CHAPTER 17

The click made him jump, but that's all it was, a simple click, not a burst. Lucas opened his eyes and found that the grimace had disappeared from Martin's face; instead, there was an angry look mixed with indignation.

"Goddamn it!" Martin cursed.

With a nimble movement, Martin seemed to split the shotgun in half and fumbled in his pockets, pulled out three cylindrical metal objects, and began to shove them into the barrel with trembling fingers. Lucas understood what was happening and came out of his trance. He leaped up the stairs, taking two steps at a time.

"Come back here!" He heard behind him, accompanied by a metallic sound.

Lucas reached the top and crossed to the right. Boom! He felt a gust of hot air on his shirt. The shot went into the wall right in front of the stairs. He reached the door with the painted flowers, pushed it, and once inside, locked it.

He glanced across the room until he found what he was looking for. At the foot of the bed, a bright orange and green object stood out: the water gun. Lucas grabbed it, removed the cap, and fought to keep his hands from shaking as he lined the mouth of the bottle with the gun's mouthpiece; his pulse hammered in his ears.

"Come here, son," Martin yelled on the other side of the door. "Come, so I can paint the walls with your blood!"

Lucas let out an involuntary shriek. He put the gun between his legs and grabbed the bottle with both hands, desperately trying to pour bleach into the gun without spilling it. The door trembled; the handle twisted wildly. Martin began to strike the wood so hard it looked as if he would push the door out of its frame—but something worse happened instead.

For a brief moment, there was silence; all noise ceased. Then, suddenly, a thundering bang shook the room. The wood splintered in all directions as a huge hole opened in the middle of the door. Lucas jumped. He looked at the water gun; barely a quarter had been filled. Please, let it be enough, he thought. He threw the empty bottle aside and put the cap back on the pistol.

A large pale hand pressed through the hole, groping for the lock. Lucas jumped to his feet, ran to the window, and pulled it up. Outside was the cold of the night and a silver crescent moon. Just below the window were the corroded roof tiles. Lucas drew the water gun and released it, hoping that it would not slip and fall into the yard below. He poked his head and arms out the window, then his torso and legs. His whole body finally got out just as Martin entered the room.

Lucas grabbed the water gun, got on his knees, and slumped against the wall. Several slabs slid to the edge as he moved, waiting for Martin to look out.

Aim a little higher than where you want to hit, his father had said, *remember that water falls in a curve.*

Although Lucas was not far from Martin, the man was a juggernaut, and Lucas had to hit him in such a small area. There was no choice; he could not fail.

“Don’t think you can run away from me!”

Lucas expected to see the muzzle of the shotgun peek out first, but was surprised to see that Martin’s torso was emerging instead, as he struggled to push his huge body through the small window. Lucas brought his water pistol to his shoulder and aimed it at Martin’s forehead.

“Hey!” Lucas yelled.

Martin turned toward the sound, and Lucas pulled the trigger several times while pulling the pump. The liquid gushed out, tracing a curve in the air, and landing on Martin’s face, first in his nose, then in his eyes and on his forehead, until his face was thoroughly soaked. Martin clawed at his eyes. The shotgun fell and hit the tiles.

“Son of a bitch! You motherfucking brat!” He shouted at the top of his lungs, shaking his head violently from side to side. “It burns! What have you done to me, you fucker? My fucking eyes!”

Lucas kicked the shotgun to one side, and it rolled down the roof and disappeared into the darkness below. Suddenly, a gigantic hand grabbed him by the neck and lifted him up. Lucas dropped the water gun helplessly. Martin clasped both hands around the boy’s neck and began to squeeze.

His throat contracting and gasping for air, Lucas kicked crazily at the giant’s chest, simultaneously gouging his nails into the man’s thick fingers; but it was in vain.

Martin’s eyes were wide, bloodshot. His face was contorted into a demon’s mask. Lucas was slipping; as his eyes began to close, he saw Martin’s face split in two. With the little strength he had left, Lucas managed to croak out one word:

"E... Eva..."

Martin stiffened, his fingers loosening enough to allow Lucas to inhale some air.

"What the fuck did you just say? How do you know that name?"

"I-I know..." Lucas tried to speak, his throat burning; he was sure he was spitting blood.

Martin blinked hard; it was evident that every blink hurt. His red eyes widened.

"You don't know anything about her," Martin breathed in an almost inaudible whisper. "So don't you dare say her name..."

Lucas spat. The saliva landed right in Martin's left eye, which had been reduced to a red basin. The big man cursed and grabbed his face with one hand. Lucas took advantage and managed to pull his neck out of the other hand. He fell with a clatter on the hard roof. A piercing pain ran down his butt and back.

Lucas slid to the edge and leaned his head down. The grass rug below was barely visible. He spotted a reflection in the bushes and noticed that it was the shotgun. From that distance, the threatening and imposing weapon looked incredibly small.

It was a considerable height. At best, he would break something. And even if he made it in one piece, where would he go? He saw nothing but trees around him. In the distance, the horizon was a pale blue strip.

Lucas turned suddenly at a grunt behind him. Martin had managed to pass through the window and was now standing, his murderous eyes fixed on him.

Lucas swallowed and jumped into the void.

CHAPTER 18

A jolt of pain ran down Lucas's leg as he landed, his weight crushing it as he hit the ground. He could hear his bone cracking clearly as if it were a dry leaf being stepped on. He twisted in the grass, screaming at the top of his lungs, with both hands on what appeared to be a new joint.

His cries of agony quickly turned to dread, as he saw Martin's massive figure fall right in front of him. The giant's boots crashed to the ground, echoing in the silence of the night. This man was indestructible, an almost supernatural force, and he was coming toward Lucas.

Lucas started crawling backward with his elbows, the stones scratching his skin like a thousand nails. He stared in horror at the over-two-hundred-pound monster that was coming to kill him. Martin's look was so frantic, so full of hatred that Lucas had to look away.

He saw a metallic glint in the bushes, and he recognized it instantly. He turned his body over, screaming in pain as he moved his leg. He propelled himself forward with his forearms and stretched out his hand until his fingers felt the cold metal.

Then Lucas turned onto his back. The shotgun weighed far more than he'd imagined, so much that it pressed into his torso, making it difficult to breathe. He put it on his shoulder the same way he'd seen Martin do it and pointed it up. Martin, who was less than two feet away, stopped short. His face was filled with fury, which slowly gave way to a grim smile.

"It has no ammo," he said.

Lucas' hands trembled. The steel grew heavier with each passing second, and he wasn't sure that his numb arms could hold out much longer. He didn't know whether or not to believe what Martin was saying. Hadn't he fired several times before having to reload the last time? Lucas tried to remember, but his mind was filled with blurry and chaotic images. How many times had Martin fired before reloading? Two, three, maybe five? Lucas hadn't been counting how many shots Martin had fired since he'd evaded him on the stairs.

"Y…you're lying," Lucas stammered.

Martin shook his head. The boy's fingers began to sag, the tip of the shotgun no longer aimed at Martin's head but at his torso. The man, however, had not moved an inch. If it was true that Martin had the game won, what was he waiting for? Why not just jump at Lucas and end it once and for all?

Lucas' gaze fell on Martin's forehead, stained with dried blood and dirt, and he saw droplets of sweat running down. The giant's eyes were fixed on him, but with an absent air; Martin was looking at him without seeing him, like an undead. And Lucas understood.

Martin was trying to remember, just like him, counting in his mind how many times he had fired the gun. This was his chance, his last chance. If Lucas really had no more ammunition, all he would do is confirm both of their suspicions, and then Martin would grab him and kill him in the most horrible way he could imagine. But if there was still a single bullet left...

Lucas said a quiet prayer, closed his eyes and put his finger on the trigger.

CHAPTER 19

The shot thrust Lucas's shoulder back with such brutality that it felt like he had dislocated it. In the darkness of his eyelids, he could discern a flash, accompanied by a thunderous roar and the flapping of frightened birds.

Lucas opened his eyes as Martin's chest exploded in a crimson flare. Chunky white lumps jutted from his torso, mingled with blood and muscles; those were his ribs, he realized. Martin took a step back, then another forward. His hands touched his chest, and he stared at them, stunned.

The smell of gunpowder penetrated Lucas' nose, his arms crumbled, and he let the shotgun fall onto his chest. Martin's face paled, and he began to sway from side to side, struggling to keep his balance.

Finally, the giant man fell forward, right on top of Lucas. The boy let out a groan as he felt the two hundred plus pounds of dead weight fall on him, his leg protesting and a knife-like pang shooting up the left side of his body; the shotgun embedded itself in his chest and pushed the air out of his lungs.

There he was, Martin, big and menacing, lying still on top of him, as if he'd just passed out drunk, the metallic scent of blood mingled with the smell of moisture and gunpowder.

Martin was dead. At last, Lucas was safe; he had survived the madhouse.

With the little air he could grasp, he found himself laughing as tears slid down his side and onto the ground. He didn't know if they were tears of happiness, fear, or relief. He didn't care. He was finally free.

His eyelids felt heavy, and he realized that he hadn't slept all night since he had been drugged. His eyes closed, and all the worries of the world vanished. He had a broken leg and was soaked in blood with a corpse on top of him. Nothing mattered anymore. He would think about what to do after he took a break, one that he deserved.

Just as his consciousness began to fade into the world of dreams, a sudden movement startled him. The next thing he knew, the hands of the corpse were wrapped around his neck.

Lucas tried to pull away, between kicks and howls. Martin only squeezed harder. Lucas's hands were caught underneath him, still holding the shotgun, but its mouth was pointing to his left; even if by some miracle he managed to move his fingers to the trigger and shoot, the bullet would probably hit a tree.

It was then, as he started to lose consciousness, that an image came to him, as clear as if he were living through it again: Martin reloading the shotgun. The man had put his finger on the back, over the trigger, and it opened in two as if it had been broken in half.

As darkness took hold, he felt a curve over the back with his forefinger. He squeezed it, and the weapon clicked open. The barrel pierced the gaping wound in Martin's chest. The giant screamed, coughing blood on Lucas' face, and his fingers loosened on Lucas' neck.

Lucas could see the life fade from Martin's eyes, who in the dim light seemed to have aged twenty years in an instant.

He gasped in some air as Martin drew in his last breath.

The old man's head fell on Lucas' shoulder. With difficulty and extreme care, he was able to push him to the side. Lucas struggled up, propping his hands and his good knee in the mud.

The darkness had dissipated, giving rise to a blue glow that flooded the house and the surrounding trees. Now that he could see clearly, he nearly broke with relief.

Lucas hobbled slowly down the dirt road until he reached the metal fence that surrounded the area. He pulled against it as hard as he could with his weakened body, barely moving it a few inches, but more than enough to squeeze through.

He stepped onto the asphalt road and looked from side to side. In the distance, a celestial image approached: flashing red and blue lights he recognized instantly. Lucas began to chuckle, which quickly turned into a fit of hysterical laughter. The police cars approached and slowed their pace. One stopped just in front of the fence and the other right in front of him. A man in a gray suit and tie emerged. He had brown eyes, wide like saucers, and a beard of a few weeks. The man kneeled in front of Lucas. His lips moved, but Lucas could not understand what he was saying; his voice sounded distant, heavenly.

"Thank you," Lucas muttered.

"It's okay. I'm agent Norman James. You're safe now."

Lucas dropped into the agent's arms and lost consciousness.

CHAPTER 20

The news did not report on the incident; the police had done an excellent job of keeping the press away. That would be better for everyone, especially for Lucas, who was now recovering from his broken leg. His friends came to the house every day to bring him the homework they had been assigned at school and to sign on the cast. Lucas appeared calm, but Mary could see something different in him, in his eyes.

Agent James didn't tell her much about it, except that they didn't have to worry about the Andersons anymore. Mary put both hands to her face and stifled a sob.

She turned off the TV and leaned back on the couch. She was sure that Lucas had seen terrible things, things that not even an adult could handle, and yet, there he was, smiling as always. Now, Lucas would say goodnight every night before bed, and he didn't need to have the lamp on anymore. Anybody who saw him would say he had improved, but Mary understood what it meant: her son had lost his innocence.

Everyone loses it, sooner or later, but her baby had lost it in such a sudden and horrifying way that she didn't know if he would be the same when he grew up; she could only pray that he would become the good man he was meant to be.

There was more. She and Tom had been keeping a secret from Lucas. With all that had happened, no matter how mature her son was, he could not know the truth. She would take it to her grave, and she knew that Tom would as well.

Lucas was adopted. He probably suspected it. After all, he was a very intelligent boy. However, if he ever realized the truth and questioned the whereabouts of his biological parents, she would lie. She would tell him that they had died in an accident or that she never knew who they were. Lucas could never know that his biological parent's surname was Anderson, that they had lost their daughter in a horrible accident, and that they had lost custody of their son—him—when he was only three years old.

The most horrible thing was not the fact that these psychopaths had kidnapped dozens of children and tortured them to death in their madhouse. Nor was the fact that they harassed Lucas as soon as they discovered where he lived, but what the agent told her when she asked about the Andersons: “Everybody in the house was dead by the time we got there.”

Lucas, her precious child, had killed his own parents.

Would you like to leave a review?

As an author, I highly appreciate the feedback I get from my readers. Reviews also help others to make an informed decision before buying. If you enjoyed this book, please consider leaving a short review.

Made in the USA
Middletown, DE
21 May 2025

75837927R00068